PERSEUS
AND THE
GORGON MEDUSA

D1386165

For Alex

PERSEUS
AND THE
GORGON MEDUSA

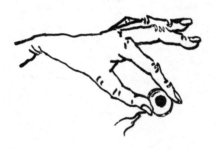

GERALDINE M^cCAUGHREAN

ILLUSTRATED BY TONY ROSS

Cavan County Library
Withdrawn Stock

ORCHARD BOOKS

CAVAN COUNTY LIBRARY
ACC. No. C.93.272......
CLASS No. ....5............
INVOICE NO. 4.3.10.16.....
PRICE..£.3.99..........

1 / JAN 2003

ORCHARD BOOKS
96 Leonard Street, London EC2A 4RH
Orchard Books Australia
14 Mars Road, Lane Cove, NSW 2066
ISBN 1 86039 438 8 (hardback)
ISBN 1 86039 531 7 (paperback)
First published in Great Britain 1997
Text © Geraldine McCaughrean 1992
Illustrations © Tony Ross 1997
1 2 3 4 5 6 02 01 00 99 98
The right of Geraldine McCaughrean to be identified as the
author and Tony Ross as the illustrator of this work has
been asserted by them in accordance with the Copyright,
Designs and Patents Act, 1988.
A CIP catalogue record for this book is available
from the British Library.
Printed in Great Britain

Long ago, when fortune-tellers told the truth, there lived a very frightened man. Like any father, King Acrisius of Argos loved his daughter, Danaë, and her baby, who was called Perseus. But one day he made the mistake of visiting a fortune-teller.

"You will be killed by Danaë's son," said the fortune-teller to the king.

CAVAN COUNTY LIBRARY

At once Acrisius gave orders for a wooden chest to be carried to the beach and set down by the water's edge.

"A chest, sire?" said his servants.

"Yes, a chest—with a lid and a big padlock. And hurry!"

Down on the beach, rough soldiers squeezed Danaë into the chest, and

tossed her baby in on top of her before slamming shut the lid.

As the chest floated out to sea, King Acrisius stood and waved it goodbye.

"They're bound to drown," he was thinking. "But I didn't kill them, did I? Nobody can say I killed them."

Instead of sinking, the chest floated. For days it floated across the sea until it was caught in the nets of a young fisherman near the shore of a faraway kingdom.

The fisherman, whose name was Dictys, took Danaë to the little wooden shack where he lived, and showed her and baby Perseus great kindness. Unfortunately, the king of that country was not as good a man as Dictys. King Polydectes liked to collect wives, as other people collect pictures. And as soon as he heard about Danaë, he wanted to add her to his collection. Danaë politely said 'no' when King Polydectes proposed to her. And she

went on saying 'no' for seventeen years.
By this time, the king was furious.

"Enough of asking nicely! Guards, go
and seize Danaë and fetch her here to
be married right away!"

He had forgotten
that after seventeen
years her son,
Perseus, had
grown into a
fine, strong
young man.
Perseus beat the
guards soundly
and sent them
back to Polydectes
all battered
and bruised.

"That Perseus is an amazing young
man, sire!" they panted. "He swears
his mother shan't marry anyone unless
she wants to. He says he'll protect her

day and night."

King Polydectes ground his teeth. "I see I must get rid of this wretched boy." So Polydectes challenged Perseus to a dare—the hardest he could imagine.

"I dare you to fetch me the head of the Gorgon Medusa," he said.

Medusa was once a beautiful but vain girl, who had made the mistake of boasting—in the gods' hearing—that no one, not even a goddess, was more beautiful than she. For her punishment, she was changed into a gorgon—a monster with glaring eyes and snakes for hair. Whoever looked at her was turned into stone.

Perseus fell right into the king's trap. "I leave at once!" he cried.

"Bravo!" cheered the courtiers. "Well said, Perseus!"

"Bravo!" thought King Polydectes. "He'll die, of course."

"Bravo!" cried the gods, looking down from Mount Olympus. "What a brave boy that Perseus is. He deserves our help."

"I'll lend him my feathered shoes," said Hermes.

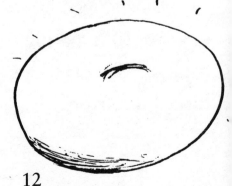

"I'll lend him my bright shield," said the goddess Athene.

"I'll lend him my helmet
of invisibility,"
said Pluto,
"and a thick bag
to put Medusa's
head in."

"I shall watch,
but not help,"
said Zeus.
"Perseus must match
his brave words with brave deeds."

A few days later, having kissed his
mother, Danaë, goodbye, Perseus set
off. He was carrying nothing more than
a sword, but soon he came across a
helmet lying in the road. He pulled the

helmet on, thinking it might be useful if he had to fight a monster. He stared down at his feet. But they had disappeared. He had no feet! Nor hands! Nor clothes, nor body! Even the helmet itself was invisible when Perseus had it on his head.

Perseus went a little further and found a shield lying in the road. Its metal was polished mirror-bright. He slung the shield over his back, thinking it might be useful if he had to fight a monster, and continued on his way.

A little further on, he found a pair of winged sandals. He buckled them on and —"Wo-wo-woah!"— found himself walking on air! Up, up, up and over the treetops the flying shoes carried him. Such sandals could not fail to be useful if he had to fight a monster. He looked up to heaven and thanked the gods for their presents, before continuing on his way to look for Medusa.

But to find her, Perseus knew he had first to find the three Grey Sisters. They alone knew where the gruesome Gorgon Medusa had her lair. These three revolting old women lived on a rocky clifftop, and kept watch for passers-by to cook in their iron cauldron. They could not all keep watch at once, though. Between the three of them, they had only one grey eye.

When he was still a long way from their den, Perseus pulled on the helmet of invisibility. As he got closer, he could hear the grisly sisters quarrelling about their supper. They could not decide whose turn it was to eat. Between the

three of them, they had only one rotten tooth.

Then one ugly sister shrieked, "My turn for the eye!"

The user of the eye sighed, and took it out of her head: "Here you are then."

"Where? Put it in my hand, why don't you?"

"I have done. Don't tell me you've dropped it."

"You never gave it me! Don't go blaming me!"

Arguing furiously, they scrabbled about, feeling for the one lost grey eye.

"I have what you are looking for," said invisible Perseus.

The Grey sisters set up a terrible wailing. "Who's that? Tear him to pieces, sister! He's stolen our precious eye!"

"Calm yourselves, ladies," said Perseus politely. "I'll give you back your eye ..."

"Good boy! Here! Give! Give! What are you waiting for!"

" ... as soon as you tell me how to find the Gorgon Medusa."

"Never! No! It's a secret!"

"Can't tell!"

"Won't tell!"

"Oh, so I can toss this eye of yours into that cauldron, can I? Or let it roll away down the mountainside?"

"No! No!"

"Don't! Don't!"

"We'll tell! We'll tell! You must travel three days east, two days north, one day west and an hour to the south. Now give us back our eye!"

The Grey Sisters crawled towards the sound of Perseus's voice, claws outstretched.

Perseus tossed the eye in among them, and left them groping for it on the rocky ground. "Don't worry, sisters," he heard one of them whisper, when they thought he had gone. "One glimpse of the Gorgon Medusa will turn that thief to stone!"

"This is a challenge fit for a hero!" thought Perseus. And he flew out eastwards over the restless sea.

Even in Hermes' winged sandals, it was a long time before Perseus spotted the Gorgon Medusa's island. It lay below him like a single grey eye in the face of the sea. He did not search about for the monster, though; he now knew that one sight of her would turn him to stone.

Instead, he found her by the sound of her hair. For he knew that instead of curls or plaits, Medusa's head was crowned with writhing, hissing snakes all spitting poison. Round about her, a hundred figures stood still as statues, turned to stone in the very moment that they had first glimpsed Medusa.

"How am I to kill this monster without looking at her?" thought Perseus.

Then the sun flashed on Athene's bright shield and gave him an idea. Holding the shield up in front of his face he flew backwards. For the first time, he was able to look at the monster, reflected in the shiny metal.

Medusa herself was asleep, though the snakes on her head never slept. They sensed that someone was nearby. They jabbed at the air with their forked tongues. But invisible Perseus kicked them aside and swung his sword in a great arc.

Medusa's hideous head fell to the ground with a thud. Only the snakes did not die. Perseus very cautiously put the head into its sack.

On the way back, as he flew over a parched desert, the Gorgon's blood dripped through the sack on to the sand below. As each drop touched the ground, a serpent wriggled away and burrowed into the sand.

As he flew home-
wards, Perseus
passed over a
country troubled
by a terrible
monster. It was
a sea serpent
which devoured
swimmers,
snatched fishermen

off the beach, and even dragged itself
ashore to grab people off the town
streets and carry them out to sea.

"What shall we do?" wailed the king.
"How can I rid my country of this
terrible danger?"

His fortune-teller said, "The gods are

angry. There is only one thing you can do. You must sacrifice your most precious possession to the sea monster. You must feed it your own daughter, Andromeda." The king howled and tore his hair, but the fortune-teller insisted: Andromeda must die.

As the guards dragged Andromeda down to the seashore, she caught sight of a handsome young friend of hers.

"Phineas! Oh, Phineas, help me! I was to be your bride. Surely you won't let them do this? Save me!"

But Phineas turned away his eyes. "They say nothing else will work. Do you want us all to be eaten in our beds, you selfish girl? You ought to be proud to do this for your country." And he hurried away with his fingers in his ears.

29

So Andromeda was chained to a
ledge on the cliff and left as a sacrifice
to the sea serpent. She looked out to
sea. Was that a giant fin cutting
through the waves? Was that a huge
tail beating the sea into a black foam?
Andromeda pulled at her chains and
screamed with all her might.

All that Perseus heard, as he flew
overhead, was a small, piping cry, like a
seagull's call. But it was enough to
make him look down. He saw the
monster speeding through the water: he
saw the girl chained against the cliff.

Like a hawk, Perseus swooped out of
the sky. But the serpent reared up out
of the water and tossed him against the

cliff. Perseus' shield fell from his shoulder, the helmet and bag fell from his grasp. He drew his sword and leapt between the princess and the monster's open mouth, and drove his sword into the beast's shoulder. Snaking its neck with pain, it lashed at him with its tail

and knocked him into the sea. To keep from drowning, Perseus clung to the only thing he could — the monster's slimy neck. Time and again he plunged in his sword. The beast writhed once, twice, three times ... then rolled over on to its back, quite dead.

When Perseus pulled himself wearily out of the water, Andromeda looked down at him with eyes full of thanks. High above, on the clifftops, the people of the country began to cheer and clap.

The news was rushed to the king, who sent for Perseus at once. "Ask any reward, young man, and you shall have it. You have saved our one and only daughter!"

"What else could I do?" said Perseus shyly. "She is so beautiful. The best reward I could ever think of is to have Andromeda for my wife."

The wedding had just begun when
Phineas arrived. He raged into the
palace with an army of fifty men.
"Where is he, this thief with the
feathery boots? How dare he steal the
girl promised to me in marriage!"

"But, Phineas! You were quite happy for me to be eaten by the sea monster!" said Andromeda. "Perseus risked his life to save mine."

"Then he won't mind dying now, will he?" sneered Phineas.

Fifty men closed in on Perseus. Each one carried a spear: each raised his arm to throw it. How could Perseus fend off fifty spears with a single sword? In the corner of the room lay the black bag. Perseus dived towards it, loosened the cords, and plunged in his hand. "All those who love Perseus, shut your eyes!" he cried, and dragged out the Gorgon Medusa's head.

Fifty spears clattered to the floor,

dropped by hands that had turned to stone. His attackers stood about like ugly statues, doomed to stand for ever with one arm lifted. Perseus quickly returned the head to its bag, for fear Andromeda should open her eyes.

Next day, with Medusa's head safely covered up and stowed away on board, bride and groom set sail for home.

With Perseus out of the way, King Polydectes thought he could force

Danaë to marry him. "Make ready for your wedding!" he commanded her. "I've wasted enough time!"

Danaë was panic-stricken. Dictys, the kind fisherman, tried to protect her, but soon five hundred soldiers surrounded Danaë and her friend.

"I've waited long enough!" declared King Polydectes. "Today shall be your wedding day, Danaë! Look. Here are five hundred ushers to bring you to the temple!" The soldiers drew their swords.

Suddenly a murmur ran through the ranks, as two people came pushing towards the king: a young man and a girl.

"I've brought you the Gorgon Medusa's head, your majesty," said Perseus. "But I see the challenge was only an excuse to get me out of the way."

King Polydectes held his sides and roared with laughter.

"Brought me the Gorgon Medusa's head? You lying little brat! Nobody could do that! Well, who cares what you really have in that sack? I'm going to marry your mother, whether you like it or not, so you may as well enjoy the wedding!"

"You don't believe me?" asked
Perseus. "Then see for yourself. See
your wedding present!" Once more he
reached into the sack. Andromeda
covered her eyes. Perseus turned aside
his head.

But Polydectes and his soldiers all stared at the thing in his hand. They stared and stared, and are staring still, still standing as they stood in that moment when the Gorgon Medusa's head turned them all to stone.

When it was all over, Perseus flew far out to sea and sank the monster's head in deep water, where it turned all the seaweed to shining coral. Then he left the magic weapons out under the evening sky, and next day they were gone.

Dictys became king in place of the wicked Polydectes, and there were great festivities because everybody liked the old fisherman. Danaë married him, and was happy at last. All the kings, queens, princes and princesses of the world gathered for the wedding and to watch a festive day of sports. There was running, jumping, wrestling, throwing the javelin ... Perseus himself put his name down for the discus-throwing contest.

When it came to his turn, he threw the brass discus much higher and harder and further than any other competitor. But the wind caught it and

spun it into the watching crowd. There
was an awful silence. An old man had
been hit! He was dead.

"Who is he? Doesn't anybody
know?" asked Perseus, tearing at his
hair with anguish.

"It is your grandfather," said Danaë

gently. "Poor man. It was his fate that you should kill him. Don't blame yourself. Nobody can cheat Fate. Do you realise what this means? Now you have a kingdom of your own! Now you are King Perseus!"

But Perseus would not rule over

Acrisius' kingdom. He was too sad at having killed his own grandfather. Instead he travelled with Andromeda to an empty land and began a new kingdom there, the noblest kingdom in all the world.

CAVAN COUNTY LIBRARY